To all of the Natural Girls around the world —MzVee

For my sisters —Lisbeth Checo

Natural Me
Text copyright © 2024 by MzVee
Illustrations copyright © 2024 by Lisbeth Checo

Library of Congress Control Number: 2023936875
ISBN 978-0-35-869521-9

The artist used mixed media (markers, colored pencils, and gouache)
to create the illustrations for this book.
Typography by Cara Llewellyn
23 24 25 26 27   RTLO   10 9 8 7 6 5 4 3 2 1

First Edition

natural me

written by MzVee   Illustrated by Lisbeth Checo

HARPER
An Imprint of HarperCollins Publishers

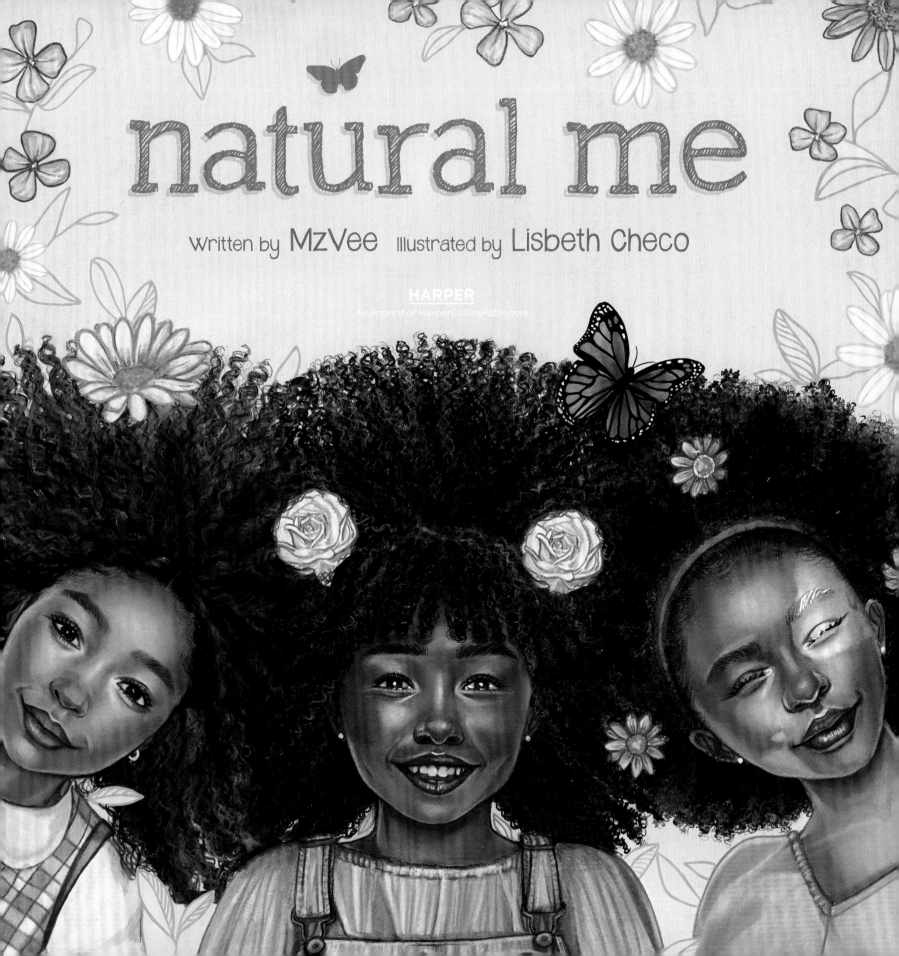

I love my hair, I love my skin.

I love the shape
that I come in.

I love my eyes, I love my nose.
I love myself from head to toes.

I am a natural girl!

The first-rate version of myself.

No imitation of someone else.

Not perfect, but perfectly me.
Loving myself and all I see.

I am a natural girl! The natural me.
The very girl I am meant to be!

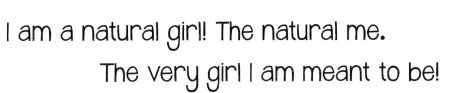

I'm beautiful in my own way.
Doesn't matter what people say.

I glitter, I sparkle, I glow.

I'm my best self, this I know.

I am a natural girl!

But although I like what I see,

I know there's so
much more to me.

Something special I cannot hide:
my real beauty is found inside.

It's the natural me!

I act with kindness and with love,
and this is what I'm most proud of.

Like a true queen,
I wear my crown
and spread my
greatness all around.

I am a natural girl!

Just my natural me.

Sharing my love and becoming the best I can be.

Not perfect, but perfectly me.

Loving myself and all I see . . .

I am a natural girl.

AUTHOR'S NOTE

Having the opportunity to write a children's book has been a very touching highlight in my career. I strive to be a voice and an outlet, teaching young girls the importance of self-LOVE and self-CARE. I've always embraced the Natural Girl, the Natural Me; it's who I am and what I'll always stand by. I hope that parents will instill these lessons of love in their children. And for every little girl reading this book, here are a few words that I want to leave you with:

Rise, young Queen, look in the mirror, and love the person you see. You have everything you need. Natural girls rule the world!